HIROSHIMA MON AMOUR

is love really as powerful as
to make you forget what
is real?

HIROSHIMA MON AMOUR

Text by
MARGUERITE DURAS

for the film by
ALAIN RESNAIS

Translated from the French
by Richard Seaver
Picture Editor: Robert Hughes

Grove Press
New York

*Originally published in 1960 by Librairie Gallimard,
Paris, France*
Printed in the United States of America

Library of Congress Catalog Card Number: 61-8011
ISBN 0-8021-3104-2

Grove Press
841 Broadway
New York, NY 10003

99 00 01   35 34 33 32 31 30 29

HIROSHIMA MON AMOUR

Produced by: *Argos-Daiei-Como-Pathe Productions*
Directed by: *Alain Resnais*
Scenario and dialogue by: *Marguerite Duras*
Directors of Photography: *Sacha Vierny and Takahashi Michio*
Music by: *Georges Delerue and Giovanni Fusco*
Settings by: *Esaka, Mayo, Petri*
Literary Adviser: *Gérard Jarlot*

The principal roles were played by Emmanuelle Riva as the French actress, and Eiji Okada as the Japanese architect.

The publishers would like to express their appreciation for the help and cooperation given by the American film distributors of *Hiroshima Mon Amour*, Zenith International Film Corporation, and its director, Mr. Dan Frankel.

PREFACE

I have tried to give as faithful an account as possible of the work I did for Alain Resnais on *Hiroshima Mon Amour.*

Readers should not be surprised that Resnais' "pictorial" contribution is practically never described in this work. My role is limited to describing those elements from which Resnais made his film.

The passages on Nevers, which were not included in the original scenario (July, 1958) were annotated before the shooting in France (December, 1958). ("Pretend you were annotating not a future film, but a finished film," Resnais told me.) They therefore represent a work apart from the script (see the Appendix: Nocturnal Notations). In the script itself only passing reference is made to them.

As I hand the book over for publication, I greatly regret that it does not include the account of the almost daily conversations between Resnais and myself, G. Jarlot and myself, and all three of us together. Their advice was always precious, and I was never able to begin work on any episode without submitting the preceding one to them and listening to their comments, which were always lucid, demanding, and productive.

Marguerite Duras

SYNOPSIS

The time is summer, 1957—August—at Hiroshima.

A French woman, about thirty years old, has come to Hiroshima to play in a film on Peace.

The story begins the day before her return to France. The film in which she's playing is practically finished. There's only one more scene to shoot.

The day before her return to France, this French woman, whose name will never be given in the film—this anonymous woman—meets a Japanese (engineer or architect) and has a very brief love affair with him.

How they met will not be revealed in the picture. For that is not what really matters. Chance meetings occur everywhere in the world. What is important is what these ordinary meetings lead to.

In the beginning of the film we don't see this chance couple. Neither her nor him. Instead we see mutilated bodies—the heads, the hips—moving—in the throes of love or death—and covered successively with the ashes, the dew, of atomic death—and the sweat of love fulfilled.

It is only by slow degrees that from these formless, anonymous bodies their own bodies emerge.

They are lying in a hotel room. Naked. Smooth bodies. Intact.

What are they talking about? About Hiroshima.

She tells him that she has seen everything in Hiroshima. We see what she has seen. It's horrible. And meanwhile his voice, a negative voice, denies the deceitful pictures, and in an impersonal, unbearable way, he repeats that she has seen nothing at Hiroshima.

Thus their initial exchange is allegorical. *In short, an operatic exchange.* Impossible to talk about Hiroshima. All one can do is talk about the impossibility of talking about Hiroshima. The knowledge of Hiroshima being stated à priori by an exemplary delusion of the mind.

This beginning, this official parade of already well-known horrors from Hiroshima, recalled in a hotel bed, this *sacrilegious* recollection, is voluntary. One can talk about Hiroshima anywhere, even in a hotel bed, during a chance, an adulterous love affair. The bodies of both protagonists, who are really in love with each other, will remind us of this. What is really sacrilegious, if anything is, is Hiroshima itself. There's no point in being hypocritical and avoiding the issue.

However little he has been shown of the *Hiroshima Monument*, these miserable remains of a *Monument of Emptiness*, the spectator should come away purged of practically all prejudice, and ready to accept anything he may be told about the two protagonists.

And at this point the film comes back to their own story.

A banal tale, one that happens thousands of times every day. The Japanese is married, has children. So is the French woman, who also has two children. Theirs is a one-night affair.

But where? At Hiroshima.

Their embrace—so banal, so commonplace—takes place in the one city of the world where it is hardest to imagine it: Hiroshima. Nothing is "given" at Hiroshima. Every gesture, every word, takes on an aura of meaning that transcends its literal meaning. And this is one of the principal goals of the film: to have done with the description of horror by horror, for that has been done by the Japanese themselves, but make this horror rise again from its ashes by incorporating it in a love that will necessarily be special and "wonderful," one that will be more credible than if it had occurred anywhere else in the world, a place that death had not *preserved.*

Between two people as dissimilar geographically, philosophically, historically, economically, racially, etc. as it is possible to be, Hiroshima will be the common ground (perhaps the only one in the world?) where the universal factors of eroticism, love, and unhappiness will appear in an implacable light. Everywhere except at Hiroshima guile is an accepted convention. At Hiroshima it cannot exist, or else it will be denounced.

Before falling asleep they talk again of Hiroshima. In a different way. With desire and, perhaps without their being aware of it, with nascent love.

Their conversation concerns both themselves and Hiroshima. And their remarks are mixed in such a way from this point on— *following the opera of Hiroshima*—that it will be impossible to distinguish one from the other.

Their personal story, however brief it may be, always dominates Hiroshima.

If this premise were not adhered to, this would be just one more made-to-order picture, of no more interest than any fictionalized documentary. If it is adhered to, we'll end up with a sort of false documentary that will probe the lesson of Hiroshima more deeply than any made-to-order documentary.

They awake. And talk again while she is getting dressed. Of ordinary things, and also of Hiroshima. Why not? It's quite natural. This is Hiroshima.

And suddenly she appears completely dressed, as a Red Cross nurse.

(This uniform, which is actually the uniform of official virtue, reawakens his desire. He wants to see her again. He's like everyone else, like all men, *exactly*, and in travesty there is an erotic factor that intrigues all men. The eternal nurse of an eternal war. . .)

Why, since she also desires him, doesn't she want to see him again? She doesn't give any clear reason.

When they awake they also talk of her past.

What happened in Nevers, her native city, in that region called Nièvre where she was brought up? What happened to make her the way she is, so free and yet so haunted, so honest and yet so dishonest, so equivocal and so clear? So predisposed to chance love affairs? So cowardly when faced with love?

One day, she tells him, one day at Nevers she was mad. Mad with spite. She says it the same way she might say that once at Nevers she saw things with perfect lucidity. The same way.

10

If that Nevers "incident" explains her present conduct at Hiroshima, she says nothing about it. She talks about the Nevers incident as she might talk about anything else. Without revealing its cause.

She leaves. She has decided not to see him again.

But they will see each other again.

Four o'clock that afternoon. Peace Square at Hiroshima (or in front of the hospital).

The cameramen are moving off (whenever we see them in the film they're moving off with their equipment). The grandstands are being dismantled. The bunting is being removed.

The French woman is asleep in the shadow (perhaps) of one of the grandstands which is being taken down.

An enlightening film about Peace has just been completed. Not at all a ridiculous film, but just another film.

A Japanese man makes his way through the crowd which, once again, presses in around the settings for the film that has just been completed. The same man we saw this morning in the hotel room. He sees the French woman, stops, goes toward her, watches her sleeping. His gaze awakens her. They exchange looks, both filled with desire. He has not come by chance. He has come to see her again.

Almost immediately after they meet, there is a parade. It's the final scene of the film. Children parading, students parading. Dogs. Cats. Idlers. All Hiroshima is there, as it always is when the cause of world peace is at stake. A *baroque* parade.

It is terribly hot. The sky is threatening. They wait for the parade to pass. As it does he tells her he thinks he loves her.

He takes her to his house. They talk briefly about their respective lives.

They're both happily married, not looking for a substitute for an unhappy marriage.

It's there, during the act of love, that she begins to tell him about Nevers.

She runs away from the house, and they go to a café overlooking the river "to kill time before her departure." Night now.

They remain there for several hours. Their love grows in inverse proportion to the time left before the plane's departure the

11

following morning.

It's here, in this café, that she tells him why she was mad in Nevers.

Her head was shaved at Nevers in 1944, when she was twenty years old. Her first lover was a German. Killed at the Liberation.

She remained in a cellar in Nevers, with her head shaved. It was only when the bomb was dropped on Hiroshima that she was presentable enough to leave the cellar and join the delirious crowd in the streets.

Why did she choose this personal sorrow? No doubt because he too is a person of extremes. To shave a girl's head because she has loved—really loved—an official enemy of her country, is the ultimate of horror and stupidity.

We see Nevers, as we've already seen it before in the hotel room. And again they talk of themselves. And once again an over-lapping of Nevers and love, of Hiroshima and love. It will all be mixed, without any preconceived principle, the way such things happen everywhere, every day, whenever couples newly in love talk.

Again she leaves. Again she runs away from him.

She tries to go back to her hotel to collect herself, doesn't suc-ceed, emerges again from the hotel and returns to the café, which by then is closed. And she stays there. Remembering Nevers (in-terior monologue), therefore love itself.

The man has followed her. She notices it. She looks at him. They look at each other, completely in love. A hopeless love, killed like the Nevers love. Therefore already relegated to obliv-ion. Therefore eternal.

And yet she doesn't join him.

She wanders through the city. *And he follows her as he would an unknown woman.* At a certain moment he accosts her and asks her to stay in Hiroshima, as if in an aside. She says no. Everyone's refusal. Common cowardice. *

For them, the die is really cast.

He doesn't insist.

She wanders to the railroad station. He joins her there. They look at each other like shadows.

From now on, nothing further to say to each other. The imminence of the departure freezes them in a funereal silence.

It's really love. All they can do now is remain silent. An ultimate scene takes place in a café. We see her there in the company of another Japanese.

And at another table the man she loves, completely motionless, his only reaction that of despair, to which he is wholly resigned but which transcends him *physically*. It is already as if she belonged to "the others." And he can only fully understand it.

At dawn she returns to her room. A few minutes later he knocks at the door. He can't help it. "Impossible not to come," he apologizes.

And in the room *nothing* happens. Both are reduced to a terrifying, mutual impotence. The room, *"the way of the world,"* remains around them, and they will disturb it no more.

No vows exchanged. No further gesture.

They simply call each other once again. What? Nevers, Hiroshima. For in fact, in each other's eyes, they *are* no one. They are names of places, names that are not names. It is as though, through them, *all of Hiroshima was in love with all of Nevers.*

She says to him: "Hiroshima, that's your name."

---

*Note: Certain spectators of the film thought she "ended up" by staying at Hiroshima. It's possible. I have no opinion. Having taken her to the limit of her refusal to stay at Hiroshima, we haven't been concerned to know whether—once the film was finished—she succeeded in reversing her refusal.

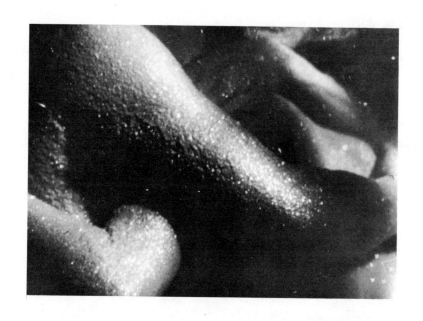

SCENARIO

Part I

(*As the film opens, two pair of bare shoulders appear, little by little. All we see are these shoulders—cut off from the body at the height of the head and hips—in an embrace, and as if drenched with ashes, rain, dew, or sweat, whichever is preferred. The main thing is that we get the feeling that this dew, this perspiration, has been deposited by the atomic "mushroom" as it moves away and evaporates. It should produce a violent, conflicting feeling of freshness and desire. The shoulders are of different colors, one dark, one light. Fusco's music accompanies this almost shocking embrace. The difference between the hands is also very marked. The woman's hand lies on the darker shoulder: "lies" is perhaps not the word; "grips" would be closer to it. A man's voice, flat and calm, as if reciting, says:*)

HE: You saw nothing in Hiroshima. Nothing.

(*To be used as often as desired. A woman's voice, also flat, muffled, monotonous, the voice of someone reciting, replies:*)

SHE: I saw *everything. Everything.*

(*Fusco's music, which has faded before this initial exchange, resumes just long enough to accompany the woman's hand tightening on the shoulder again, then letting go, then caressing it. The mark of fingernails on the darker flesh. As if this scratch could give the illusion of being a punishment for: "No. You saw nothing in Hiroshima." Then the woman's voice begins again, still calm, colorless, incantatory:*)

SHE: The hospital, for instance, I saw it. I'm sure I did. There is a hospital in Hiroshima. How could I help seeing it?

15

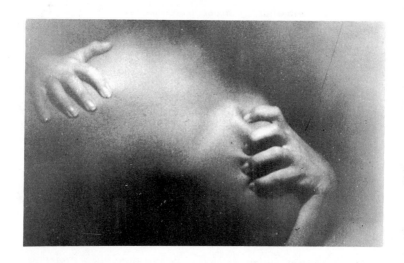

(The hospital, hallways, stairs, patients, the camera coldly objective.° [We never see her seeing.] *Then we come back to the hand gripping—and not letting go of—the darker shoulder.)*

HE: You did not see the hospital in Hiroshima. You saw nothing in Hiroshima.

(Then the woman's voice becomes more . . . more impersonal. Shots of the museum.† The same blinding light, the same ugly light here as at the hospital. Explanatory signs, pieces of evidence from the bombardment, scale models, mutilated iron, skin, burned hair, wax models, etc.)

SHE: Four times at the museum. . . .

HE: What museum in Hiroshima?

SHE: Four times at the museum in Hiroshima. I saw the people walking around. The people walk around, lost in thought, among the photographs, the reconstructions, for want of something else, among the photographs, the photographs, the reconstructions, for want of something else, the explanations, for want of something else.

Four times at the museum in Hiroshima.

I looked at the people. I myself looked thoughtfully at the iron. The burned iron. The broken iron, the iron made vulnerable as flesh. I saw the bouquet of bottle caps: who would have suspected that? Human skin floating, surviving, still in the bloom of its agony. Stones. Burned stones. Shattered stones. Anonymous heads of hair that the women of Hiroshima, when they awoke in the morning, discovered had fallen out.

I was hot at Peace Square. Ten thousand degrees at Peace Square. I know it. The temperature of the sun at Peace Square. How can you not know it? . . . The grass, it's quite simple. . .

°With only a schematic initial text to go on, Resnais brought back a great number of documents from Japan. Thus the initial text was modified and considerably enlarged during the cutting of the film.

†With a return, at regular intervals, to the bodies.

HE: You saw nothing in Hiroshima. Nothing.

(More shots of the museum. Then a shot of Peace Square taken with a burned skull in the foreground. Glass display cases with burned models inside. Newsreel shots of Hiroshima.)

SHE: The reconstructions have been made as authentically as possible.

The films have been made as authentically as possible.

The illusion, it's quite simple, the illusion is so perfect that the tourists cry.

One can always scoff, but what else can a tourist do, really, but cry?

I've always wept over the fate of Hiroshima. Always.

(A panorama of a photograph taken of Hiroshima after the bomb, a "new desert" without reference to the other deserts of the world.)

HE: No. What would you have cried about?

(Peace Square, empty under a blinding sun that recalls the blinding light of the bomb. Newsreels taken after August 6, 1945. Ants, worms, emerge from the ground. Interspersed with shots of the shoulders. The woman's voice begins again, gone mad, as the sequence of pictures has also gone mad.)

SHE: I saw the newsreels.

On the second day, History tells, I'm not making it up, on the second day certain species of animals rose again from the depths of the earth and from the ashes.

Dogs were photographed.

For all eternity.

I saw them.

I *saw* the newsreels.

I *saw* them.

On the first day.

On the second day.

On the third day.

HE *(interrupting her)*: You saw nothing. Nothing.

(A dog with a leg amputated. People, children. Wounds. Burned children screaming.)

SHE: . . . on the fifteenth day too.

Hiroshima was blanketed with flowers. There were cornflowers and gladiolas everywhere, and morning glories and day lilies that rose again from the ashes with an extraordinary vigor, quite unheard of for flowers till then.*

I didn't make anything up.

HE: You made it *all* up.

SHE: *Nothing.*

Just as in love this illusion exists, this illusion of being able never to forget, so I was under the illusion that I would never forget Hiroshima.

Just as in love.

---

*This sentence is taken almost verbatim from John Hersey's admirable report on Hiroshima. All I did was apply it to the martyred children.

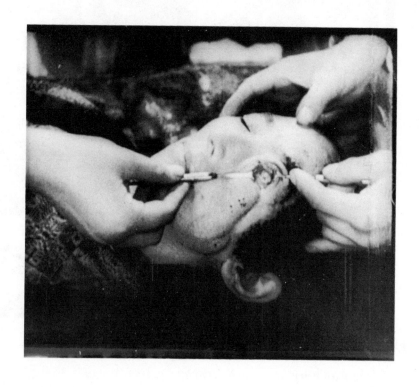

(Surgical forceps approach an eye to extract it. More newsreel shots.)

I also saw the survivors and those who were in the wombs of the women of Hiroshima.

(Shots of various survivors: a beautiful child who, upon turning around, is blind in one eye; a girl looking at her burned face in the mirror; a blind girl with twisted hands playing the zither; a woman praying near her dying children; a man, who has not slept for several years, dying. [Once a week they bring his children to see him.])

I saw the patience, the innocence, the apparent meekness with which the temporary survivors of Hiroshima adapted themselves to a fate so unjust that the imagination, normally so fertile, cannot conceive it.

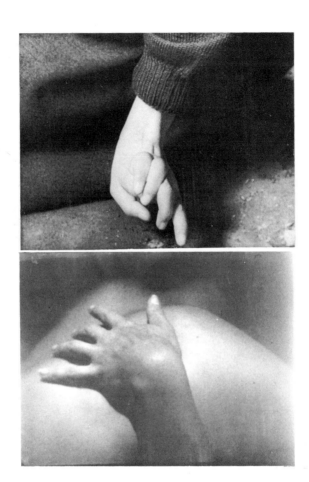

(And again a return to the perfect embrace of the bodies.)

Listen. . .
I know. . .
I know *everything*.
It went on.

HE: *Nothing. You know nothing.*

(A spiraling atomic cloud. People marching in the streets in the rain. Fishermen tainted with radioactivity. Unedible fish. Thousands of unedible fish buried.)

SHE: Women risk giving birth to malformed children, to monsters, but it goes on.

Men risk becoming sterile, but it goes on.

People are afraid of the rain.

The rain of ashes on the waters of the Pacific.

The waters of the Pacific kill.

Fishermen of the Pacific are dead.

People are afraid of the food.

The food of an entire city is thrown away.

The food of entire cities is buried.

An entire city rises up in anger.

Entire cities rise up in anger.

(Newsreels: demonstrations.)

Against whom, the anger of entire cities?

The anger of entire cities, whether they like it or not, against the inequality set forth as a principle by certain people against other people, against the inequality set forth as a principle by certain races against other races, against the inequality set forth as a principle by certain classes against other classes.

(Processions of demonstrators. "Mute" speeches from loudspeakers.)

SHE *(softly)*: . . . Listen to me.

Like you, I know what it is to forget.

acid rain

HE: No, you don't know what it is to forget.

SHE: Like you, I have a memory. I know what it is to forget.

HE: No, you don't have a memory.

SHE: Like you, I too have tried with all my might not to forget. Like you, I forgot. Like you, I wanted to have an inconsolable memory, a memory of shadows and stone.

(The shot of a shadow, "photographed" on stone, of someone killed at Hiroshima.)

For my part, I struggled with all my might, every day, against the horror of no longer understanding at all the reason for remembering. Like you, I forgot. . . .

(Shops with hundreds of scale models of the Palace of Industry, the only monument whose twisted skeleton remained standing after the bomb—and was afterward preserved. An empty shop. A busload of Japanese tourists. Tourists on Peace Square. A cat crossing Peace Square.)

Why deny the obvious necessity for memory? . . .

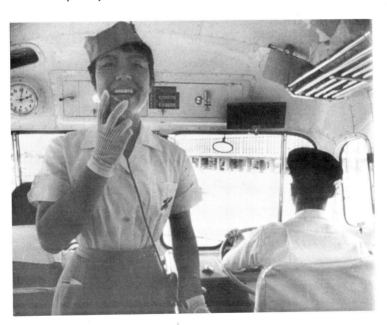

(A sentence punctuated by shots of the framework of the Palace of Industry.)

. . . Listen to me. I know something else. It will begin all over again.

Two hundred thousand dead.

Eighty thousand wounded.

In nine seconds. These figures are official. It will begin all over again.

(Trees. Church. Merry-go-round. Hiroshima rebuilt. Banality.)

There will be ten thousand degrees on the earth. Ten thousand suns, they will say. The asphalt will burn.

(Church. Japanese advertising poster.)

Chaos will prevail. A whole city will be raised from the earth and fall back in ashes. . . .

(Sand. A package of "Peace" cigarettes. A fat plant spread out like a spider on the sand.)

New vegetation will rise from the sands. . . .

(Four "dead" students chat beside the river. The river. The tides. The daily piers of Hiroshima rebuilt.)

Four students await together a fraternal and legendary death.

The seven branches of the delta estuary in the Ota river drain and fill at the usual hour, exactly at the usual hours, with water that is fresh and rich with fish, gray or blue depending on the hour or the season. Along the muddy banks people no longer watch the tide rising slowly in the seven branches of the delta estuary of the river Ota.

(The incantatory tone ceases. The streets of Hiroshima, more streets. Bridges. Covered lanes. Streets. Suburbs. Railroad tracks. Suburbs. Universal banality.)

SHE: . . . I meet you.

I remember you.

24

Who are you?

You destroy me.

You're so good for me.

How could I have known that this city was made to the size of love?

How could I have known that you were made to the size of my body?

You're great. How wonderful. You're great.

How slow all of a sudden.

And how sweet.

More than you can know.

You destroy me.

You're so good for me.

You destroy me.

You're so good for me.

Plenty of time.

Please.

Take me.

Deform me, make me ugly.

Why not you?

Why not you in this city and in this night so like the others you can't tell the difference?

Please. . .

(With exaggerated suddenness the woman's face appears, filled with tenderness, turned toward the man's.)

SHE: It's extraordinary how beautiful your skin is.

(He sighs.)

You. . .

(His face appears. He laughs ecstatically, which has nothing to do with their words. He turns.)

HE: Yes, me. You will have seen me.

(The two naked bodies reappear. Same voice of the woman, muted, but this time not declamatory.)

SHE: Are you completely Japanese or aren't you completely Japanese?

25

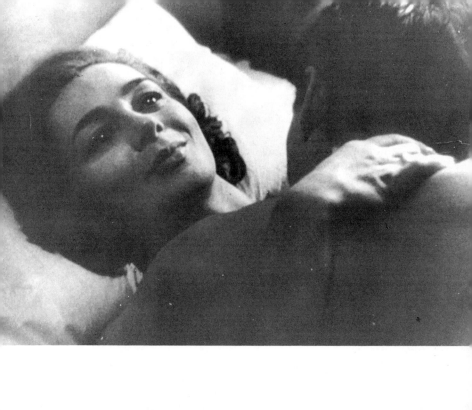
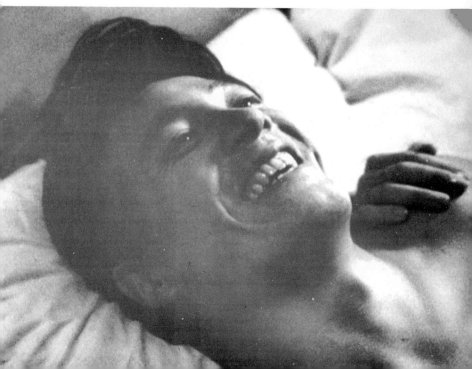

HE: Completely. I am Japanese.

You're eyes are green. Correct?

SHE: I think so . . . yes . . . I think they're green.

HE *(softly, looking at her):* You are like a thousand women in one. . . .

SHE: It's because you don't know me. That's why.

HE: Perhaps that's not the only reason.

SHE: It's a rather nice idea, being a thousand women in one for you.

(She kisses his shoulder and snuggles into the hollow of that shoulder. Her head is facing the open window, facing Hiroshima, the night. A man passes in the street and coughs. [We don't see him, only hear him.] She raises herself.)

SHE: Listen. . . . It's four o'clock. . . .

HE: Why?

SHE: I don't know who it is. Every day he passes at four o'clock. And he coughs.

(Silence. They look at each other.)

You were here, at Hiroshima. . . .

HE *(laughing, as he might at a childish question)*: No. . . Of course I wasn't.

SHE *(caressing his naked shoulder again)*: That's true. . . . How stupid of me. *(Almost smiling.)*

HE *(serious, hesitant)*: But my family was at Hiroshima. I was off fighting the war.

SHE *(timidly, smiling now)*: A stroke of luck, eh?

HE *(not looking at her, weighing the pro and con)*: Yes.

SHE: Lucky for me too.

(Pause.)

HE: What are you doing at Hiroshima?

SHE: A film.

HE: What, a film?

SHE: I'm playing in a film.

HE: And before coming to Hiroshima, where were you?

SHE: In Paris.

(A longer pause.)

HE: And before Paris? . . .

SHE: Before Paris? . . . I was at Nevers. *Ne-vers.*

HE: Nevers?

SHE: It's in the province of Nièvre. You don't know it.

(Pause. Then he asks, as though he had just discovered a link between Hiroshima and Nevers:)

HE: And why did you want to see everything at Hiroshima?

SH *(trying to be sincere)*: Because it interested me. I have my own ideas about it. For instance, I think looking closely at things is something that has to be learned.

Part II

(A swarm of bicycles passes in the street, the noise growing louder, then fading. She is on the balcony of the hotel, in a dressing gown. She is looking at him. She holds a cup of coffee in her hand. He is still asleep, lying on his stomach, his arms crossed, bare to the waist.

She looks very intently at his hands, which tremble slightly, as children's hands do sometimes when they are asleep. He has very beautiful, very virile hands.

While she is looking at them, there suddenly appears, in place of the Japanese, the body of a young man, lying in the same position, but in a posture of death, on the bank of a river, in full daylight. [The room is in semi-darkness.] The young man is near death. He too has beautiful hands, strikingly like those of the Japanese. The approach of death makes them jerk violently.

The shot is an extremely brief one.

She remains frozen, leaning against the window. He awakes and smiles at her. She doesn't return his smile immediately. She continues to look at him attentively, without moving. Then she takes the coffee over to him.)

SHE: Do you want some coffee?

(He assents, takes the cup. Pause.)

SHE: What were you dreaming about?

HE: I don't remember. . . . Why?

(She has become herself again, extremely nice.)

SHE: I was looking at your hands. They move when you're asleep.

HE (examining his hands, perhaps moving his fingers): Maybe it's when you dream without knowing it.

SHE (calmly, pleasantly, but seeming to doubt his words): Hmm, hmm.

29

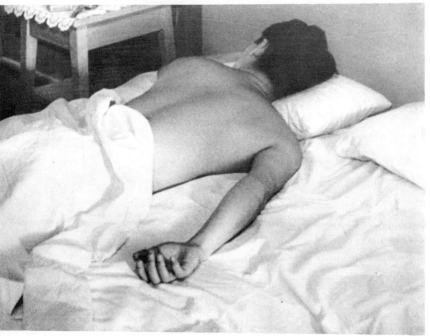

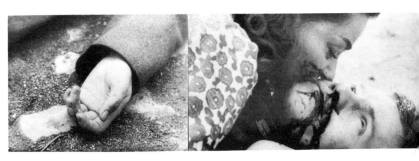

(They're together in the shower of the hotel room. In a gay mood. He puts his hand on her forehead and arches her head back.)

HE: You're a beautiful woman, do you know that?

SHE: Do you think so?

HE: I think so.

SHE: A trifle worn out, no?

HE *(laughing)*: A trifle ugly.

SHE *(smiling at his caress)*: Don't you mind?

HE: That's what I noticed last night in that café. The way you're ugly. And also. . .

SHE *(very relaxed)*: And also? . . .

HE: And also how bored you were.

SHE *(her curiosity aroused)*: Tell me more. . . .

HE: You were bored in a way that makes men want to know a woman.

SHE *(smiling, lowering her eyes)*: You speak French very well.

HE *(gaily)*: Don't I though! I'm glad you finally noticed how well I speak French. *(Pause.)* I hadn't noticed that you didn't

32

speak Japanese. . . . Have you ever noticed that it's always in the same sense that people notice things?

SHE: No. I noticed you, that's all.

(Laughter.)

(After the bath. Her hair is wet. She is munching slowly on an apple. She is on the balcony, dressed in a bathrobe; she looks at him, stretches, and as if to "pinpoint" their situation, says slowly, as though savoring the words:)

SHE: To-meet-in-Hiroshima. It doesn't happen every day.

(Already dressed—his shirt collar open—he joins her on the balcony and sits down opposite her. After a moment's hesitation, he asks:)

HE: What did Hiroshima mean for you, in France?

SHE: The end of the war, I mean, really the end. Amazement . . . at the idea that they had dared . . . amazement at the idea that they had succeeded. And then too, for us, the beginning of an unknown fear. And then, indifference. And also the fear of indifference. . . .

HE: Where were you?

SHE: I had just left Nevers. I was in Paris. In the street.

HE: That's a pretty French word, Nevers.

SHE *(after a pause)*: It's a word like any other. Like the city.

(She moves away. They begin to talk, about ordinary things.)

(He's seated on the bed; he lights a cigarette, looks at her intently, then asks:)

HE: Have you met many Japanese at Hiroshima?

SHE: I've met some, yes . . . but no one like you. . . .

HE *(smiling, gay)*: I'm the first Japanese in your life?

SHE: Yes.

(Her laughter off-camera. She reappears while she is getting dressed.)

SHE: Hi-ro-shi-ma.

HE *(lowering his eyes, calmly)*: The whole world was happy. You were happy with the whole world. *(Continuing, in the same tone:)* I heard it was a beautiful summer day in Paris that day, is that right?

SHE: Yes, it was a beautiful day.

HE: How old were you?

SHE: Twenty. And you?

HE: Twenty-two.

SHE: The same age, really.

HE: Yes, practically.

(She appears completely dressed, just as she is putting on her Red Cross nurse's kerchief. She bends down beside him with a sudden gesture, or lies down beside him. She plays with his hand, kisses his bare arm. They talk about ordinary things.)

SHE: What do you do in life?

HE: Architecture. And politics too.

SHE: Oh, so that's why you speak such good French.

HE: That's why. To read about the French Revolution.

(They laugh. Any precise indications about his politics would be absolutely impossible, since he would be immediately tagged. And besides, it would be naive. Nor should it be forgotten that only a man of liberal opinions would have made the preceding remark.)

HE: What's the film you're playing in?

SHE: A film about Peace. What else do you expect them to make in Hiroshima except a picture about Peace?

(A noisy swarm of bicycles passes.)

HE: I'd like to see you again.

34

SHE *(gesturing negatively)*: At this time tomorrow I'll be on my way back to France.

HE: Is that true? You didn't tell me.

SHE: It's true. *(Pause.)* There was no point in telling you.

HE *(serious, taken aback)*: Is that why you let me come up to your room last night? . . . Because it was your last day at Hiroshima?

SHE: Not at all. The thought never even crossed my mind.

HE: When you talk, I wonder whether you lie or tell the truth.

SHE: I lie. And I tell the truth. But I don't have any reason to lie to you. Why? . . .

HE: Tell me . . . do things like . . . this happen to you often?

SHE: Not very often. But it happens. I have a weakness for men. *(Pause.)* I have doubtful morals, you know. *(She laughs.)*

HE: What do you call having doubtful morals?

SHE: Being doubtful about the morals of other people.

(He laughs heartily.)

HE: I'd like to see you again. Even if the plane is leaving tomorrow. Even if you do have doubtful morals.

(Pause. A feeling of love returning.)

SHE: No.

HE: Why?

SHE *(with irritation)*: Because.

(He doesn't pursue the conversation.)

SHE: Don't you want to talk to me any more?

HE *(after a pause)*: I'd like to see you again.

(They are in the hotel corridor.)

HE: Where are you going in France? To Nevers?

SHE: No. To Paris. *(A pause.)* I don't ever go to Nevers any more.

HE: Not ever?

SHE *(grimacing as she says it)*: Not ever. *(Then, caught in her own trap, she adds:)* In Nevers I was younger than I've ever been. . . .

HE: Young-in-Nevers.

SHE: Yes. Young in Nevers. And then too, once, mad in Nevers.

(They are pacing back and forth in front of the hotel. She is waiting for the car that is supposed to come and pick her up to take her to Peace Square. Few people, but lots of cars passing. It's a boulevard. The dialogue is almost shouted because of the noise of the cars.)

SHE: You see, Nevers is the city in the world, and even the thing in the world, I dream about most often at night. And at the same time it's the thing I think about the least.

HE: What was your madness like at Nevers?

SHE: Madness is like intelligence, you know. You can't explain it. Just like intelligence. It comes on you, it fills you, and then you understand it. But when it goes away you can't understand it at all any longer.

HE: Were you full of hate?

SHE: That was what my madness was. I was mad with hate. I had the impression it would be possible to make a real career of hate. All I cared about was hate. Do you understand?

HE: Yes.

SHE: It's true. I suppose you must understand that too.

HE: Did it ever happen to you again?

SHE: No. *(In a near whisper:)* It's all over.

HE: During the war?

SHE: Right after it.

(Pause.)

HE: Was that part of the difficulties of life in France after the war?

SHE: Yes, that's one way of putting it.

HE: When did you get over your madness?

SHE *(in a low voice, as she would talk in normal circumstances)*: It went away little by little. And then of course when I had children.

(The noise of the cars grows and fades in inverse proportion to the seriousness of their remarks.)

HE: What did you say?

SHE: I said it went away little by little. And then of course when I had children. . . .

HE: I'd really like to spend a few days with you somewhere, sometime.

SHE: I would too.

HE: Seeing you again today wouldn't really be seeing you again. You can't see people again in such a short time. I really would.

SHE: No.

(She stops in front of him, obstinate, motionless, silent. He almost accepts.)

HE: All right.

(She laughs, but it's a little forced. She seems slightly, but actually, spiteful. The taxi arrives.)

SHE: It's because you know I'm leaving tomorrow.

(They laugh, but his is less hearty than hers. A pause.)

HE: It's possible that's part of it. But that's as good a reason as any, no? The thought of not seeing you again . . . ever . . . in a few hours.

(The taxi has arrived and stopped at the intersection. She signals to it that she's coming. She takes her time, looks at the Japanese, and says:)

SHE: No.

(His eyes follow her. Perhaps he smiles.)

Part III

(It's four P.M. *at Peace Square in Hiroshima. In the distance a group of film technicians is moving away carrying a camera, lights, and reflectors. Japanese workers are dismantling the official grandstand that has just been used in the last scene of the film.*

An important note: we will always see the technicians in the distance and will never know what film it is they're shooting at Hiroshima. All we'll ever see is the scenery being taken down.

*Stagehands are carrying posters in various languages—Japanese French, German, etc.—*NEVER ANOTHER HIROSHIMA. *The workmen are thus busy dismantling the official grandstands and removing the bunting. On the set we see the French woman. She is asleep. Her nurse's kerchief has slipped partly off her head. She is lying in the shadow of one of the stands.*

We gather that they have just finished shooting an enlightening film on Peace at Hiroshima. It's not necessarily a ridiculous film, merely an enlightening one. A crowd passes along the square where they have just been shooting the film. The crowd is indifferent. Except for a few children, no one looks, they are used to seeing films being shot at Hiroshima.

But one man passes, stops, and looks, the man we had seen previously in her hotel room. He approaches the nurse, and watches her sleeping. His gaze is what finally wakes her up, but only after he has been looking at her for a good while.

During the scene perhaps we see a few details in the distance, such as a scale model of the Palace of Industry, a guide surrounded by tourists, a couple of war invalids in white, begging, a family chatting on a street corner. She awakes. Her fatigue vanishes. They suddenly find themselves involved again with their own story. This personal story always dominates the necessarily demonstrative Hiroshima story.

She gets up and goes toward him. He laughs, a bit stiffly. Then they become serious again.)

HE: It was easy to find you in Hiroshima.

(She laughs happily. A pause. He looks at her again. Two workers —carrying an enlarged photograph from the picture The Children of Hiroshima *showing a dead mother and a child crying in the smoking ruins of Hiroshima—pass between them. They don't look at the photograph. Another photograph, of Einstein, follows immediately after the one of the mother and child.)*

HE: Is it a French film?

SHE: No. International. On Peace.

HE: Is it finished?

SHE: Yes, for me it's finished. They still have some crowd scenes to shoot. . . . We have lots of filmed commercials to sell soap. So . . . by stressing it . . . perhaps.

HE *(with very clear ideas on the subject)*: Yes, by stressing it. Here, at Hiroshima, we don't joke about films on Peace.

(He turns back toward her. The photographs have gone completely by. Instinctively they move closer together. She readjusts her kerchief, which has slipped partly off while she was sleeping.)

HE: Are you tired?

SHE *(looking at him in a way that is both provocative and gentle. Then, with an almost sad smile, she says)*: No more than you are.

HE *(meaningfully)*: I thought of Nevers in France.

(She smiles.)

HE: I've been thinking of you. Is your plane still leaving tomorrow?

SHE: Still tomorrow.

HE: Irrevocably tomorrow?

SHE: Yes. The picture is behind schedule. I'm a month overdue returning to Paris.

(She looks squarely at him. Slowly he takes her kerchief off. Either she is very heavily made up, in which case her lips are so dark they seem black, or else she is hardly made up at all and seems pale under the sun.

The man's gesture is extremely free, composed, producing much the same erotic shock as in the opening scenes. Her hair is as mussed as it was in bed the night before. She lets him take off her kerchief, she lets him have his way as she must have let him have his way in love the night before. [Here, give him an erotically functional role.]

She lowers her eyes. An incomprehensible pout. She toys with something on the ground, then raises her eyes again.)

HE: You give me a great desire to love.

(She doesn't answer right away. His words upset her, and she lowers her eyes again. The cat of Peace Square rubbing against her foot?)

SHE *(slowly)*: Always . . . chance love affairs. . . . Me too.

(Some extraordinary object, not clearly defined, passes between them. I see a square frame, some [atomic?] very precise form, but without the least idea what it's used for. They pay no attention to it.)

HE: No. Not always like this. You know it.

(Shouts in the distance. Then children singing. But it doesn't distract them. She makes an incomprehensible face [licentious would be the word]. She raises her eyes again, but this time to the sky, and says, again incomprehensibly, as she wipes the sweat from her forehead:)

SHE: They say there'll be a thunderstorm before nightfall.

(A shot of the sky she sees. Clouds scudding. . . The singing becomes more distinct. Then [the end of] the parade begins.
They back away. She clings to him [like the postures in women's magazines], her hand on his shoulder. His face against her hair. When she raises her eyes she sees him. He'll try and lead her away from the parade. She'll resist. But she'll go anyway, without realizing she's leaving.
Children parading carrying posters.)

FIRST SERIES OF POSTERS

1st Poster
If 14 A-bombs equal 100 million ordinary bombs.
2nd Poster
And if the H-bomb equals 1500 A-bombs.
3rd Poster
How much do the 40,000 A- and H-bombs actually manufactured in the world equal?
4th Poster
10 H-bombs dropped on the world mean prehistory again.
5th Poster
What do 40,000 H- and A-bombs mean?

SECOND SERIES OF POSTERS

I

This extraordinary achievement bears witness to man's scientific inteligence.[*]

II

But it's regrettable that man's political intelligence is 100 times less developed than his scientific intelligence.

III

Which keeps us from really admiring man.

---

[*]Resnais decided to leave in the error in spelling.

(*Men, women, follow the singing children. Dogs follow the children. Cats at the windows. [The Peace Square cat is used to it, and is asleep.]*
Posters. More posters. Everyone very hot.The sky, above the parade, is threatening. Clouds cover the sun. There are lots of children, beautiful children. They are hot, and sing heartily as children will. Irresistibly, and almost without realizing it, the Japanese pushes the French woman in the same—or in the opposite—direction the parade is moving. She closes her eyes and sighs, and while she is sighing:)

HE: I hate to think about your leaving. Tomorrow. I think I love you.

(*He buries his lips in her hair. Her hand tight on his shoulder. Slowly her eyes open. The parade goes on. The children's faces are made up white. Dots of sweat stand out on the white powder. Two of them argue over an orange, angrily. A man, made up as if burned in the bombing, passes. He probably had played in the film. The wax on his neck melts and falls off. Perhaps disgusting, terrifying. They look at each other.*)

HE: You're coming with me, once more.

(*She doesn't answer. A beautiful Japanese woman, sitting on a float, passes. She looses a flock of pigeons [or maybe some other*

43

allegorical float—an atomic ballet, for instance].)

HE: Answer me.

(She doesn't answer. He bends and whispers in her ear.)

HE: Are you afraid?

SHE *(smiling, shaking her head)*: No.

(The formless songs of the children continue, but fading away. A monitor scolds the two children arguing over the orange. The big one takes the orange. The big one begins to eat the orange. All this lasts longer than it should. Behind the crying child, the five hundred Japanese students arrive. It's a little terrifying, and he pulls her against him. They look upset. He looking at her, she

looking at the parade. One should have the feeling that this parade is depriving them of the short time they have left. They are silent. He leads her by the hand. She lets him. They exit, moving against the current of the parade. We lose sight of them.*)

---

*Resnais has them get lost in the crowd.

(*We see them next in the middle of a large room in a Japanese house. Soft light. A feeling of freshness after the heat of the parade. A modern house, with chairs, etc. She stands there, like a guest. Almost intimidated. He approaches her from the far side of the room [as if he had just closed the door, or come from the garage, etc.].*)

HE: Sit down.

(*She doesn't sit down. Both remain standing. We feel that eroticism is held in check between them by love, at least for the moment. He is facing her. And in the same state, almost awkward. The opposite of what a man would do if this were an* aubaine.)

SHE (*making conversation*): You're alone at Hiroshima? . . . Where's your wife?

HE: She's at Unzen, in the mountains. I'm alone.

SHE: When is she coming back?

HE: In a few days.

45

SHE (*softly, as if in an aside*): What is your wife like?

HE (*purposefully*): Beautiful. I'm a man who's happy with his wife.

(*Pause.*)

SHE: So am I. I'm a woman who's happy with her husband.

(*This exchange charged with real emotion, which the ensuing moment covers.*)

SHE: Don't you work in the afternoon?

HE: Yes. A lot. Mainly in the afternoon.

SHE: The whole thing is stupid. . . .

(*As she would say "I love you." They kiss as the telephone rings. He doesn't answer.*)

SHE: Is it because of me you're wasting your afternoon?

(*He still doesn't answer the phone.*)

SHE: Tell me. What difference does it make?

(At Hiroshima. The light is already different. Later. After they have made love.)

HE: Was he French, the man you loved during the war?

(At Nevers. A German crosses a square at dusk.)

SHE: No . . . he wasn't French.

(At Hiroshima. She is lying on the bed, pleasantly tired. Darker now.)

SHE: Yes. It was at Nevers.

(Nevers. A shot of love at Nevers. Bicycles racing. The forest, etc.)

SHE: At first we met in barns. Then among the ruins. And then in rooms. Like anywhere else.

(Hiroshima. In the room, the light has faded even more. Their bodies in a peaceful embrace.)

SHE: And then he was dead.

(Nevers. Shots of Nevers. Rivers. Quays. Poplar trees in the wind, etc. The quay deserted. The garden. Then at Hiroshima again.)

SHE: I was eighteen and he was twenty-three.

(Nevers. In a "hut" at night. The "marriage" at Nevers. During the shots of Nevers she answers the questions that he is presumed to have asked, but doesn't out loud. The sequence of shots of Nevers continues. Then:)

SHE *(calmly)*: Why talk of him rather than the others?

HE: Why not?

SHE: No. Why?

HE: Because of Nevers. I can only begin to know you, and among the many thousands of things in your life, I'm choosing Nevers.

SHE: Like you'd choose anything else?

HE: Yes.

(Do we know he's lying? We suspect it. She becomes almost violent, searching for something to say:)

SHE: No, it's not by chance. *(Pause.)* You have to tell me why.

(He can reply—a very important point for the film—either:)

HE: It was there, I seem to have understood, that you were so young . . . so young you still don't belong to anyone in particular. I like that.

(or:)

SHE: No, that's not it.

HE: It was there, I seem to have understood, that I almost . . . lost you . . . and that I risked never knowing you.

(or else:)

HE: It was there, I seem to have understood, that you must have begun to be what you are today.

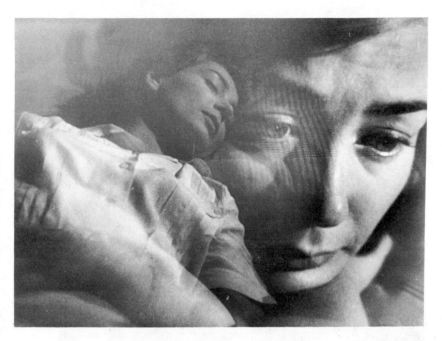

(Choose from among the three possibilities, or use all three, either one after the other, or separately, at random with the movements of love in the bed. The last is the solution I would prefer, if it doesn't make the scene too long.*
One last time we come back to them.)

SHE *(shouting)*: I want to leave here. *(She clings to him almost savagely.)*

(They are dressed and in the same room where they were earlier. The lights are on now. They are both standing.)

HE *(very calmly)*: All we can do now is kill the time left before your departure. Still sixteen hours before your plane leaves.

SHE *(terribly upset, distressed)*: That's a terribly long time. . . .

HE *(gently)*: No. You mustn't be afraid.

---

*Instead of using only one, Resnais decided to use all three.

Part IV

(Night falls over Hiroshima, leaving long trails of light. The river drains and fills with the hours, the tides. Sometimes people along the muddy banks watch the tide rising slowly.

Opposite this river is a café. A modern café, Americanized, with a wide bay window. Those seated at the back of the café don't see the banks of the river, but only the river itself. The mouth of the river is only vaguely outlined. There Hiroshima ends and the Pacific begins. The place is half empty. They are seated at a table in the back of the room, facing each other, either cheek-to-cheek, or forehead against forehead. In the previous scene they had been overwhelmed by the thought that their final separation was only sixteen hours away. When we see them now they are almost happy. They don't notice the time passing. A miracle has occurred. What miracle? The resurrection of Nevers. And in this posture of hopelessly happy love, he says:)

HE: Aside from that, Nevers doesn't mean anything else in French?

SHE: No. Nothing.

HE: Would you have been cold in that cellar at Nevers, if we had loved each other there?

SHE: I would have been cold. In Nevers the cellars are cold, both summer and winter. The city is built along a river called the Loire.

HE: I can't picture Nevers.

(Shots of Nevers. The Loire.)

SHE: Nevers. Forty thousand inhabitants. Built like a capital— (but). A child can walk around it. *(She moves away from him.)* I was born in Nevers *(she drinks)*, I grew up in Nevers. I learned how to read in Nevers. And it was there I became twenty.

HE: And the Loire?

(He takes her head in his hands. Nevers.)

SHE: It's a completely unnavigable river, always empty, because
of its irregular course and its sand bars. In France, the Loire
is considered a very beautiful river, especially because of its
light . . . so soft, if you only knew.

(Ecstatic tone. He frees her head and listens closely.)

HE: When you are in the cellar, am I dead?

SHE: You are dead . . . and . . .

(Nevers: the German is dying very slowly on the quay.)

SHE: . . . how is it possible to bear such pain?
The cellar is small.

*(To show with her hands how small it is, she withdraws her cheek
from his. Then she goes on, still very close to him, but no longer
touching him. No incantation. She speaks to him with passionate
enthusiasm.)*

SHE: . . . very small. The *Marseillaise* passes above my head. It's . . . deafening. . . .

(*She blocks her ears, in this café [at Hiroshima]. The café is suddenly very quiet. Shots of Nevers' cellars. Riva's bloody hands.*)

SHE: Hands become useless in cellars. They scrape. They rub the skin off . . . against the walls . . .

(*Somewhere at Nevers, bleeding hands. Hers, on the table, are intact. Riva licks her own blood.*)

SHE: . . . that's all you can find to do, to make you feel better . . . and also to remember . . . I loved blood since I had tasted yours.

(*They scarcely look at each other as she talks. They look at Nevers. Both of them act as if they were somehow possessed by Nevers. There are two glasses on the table. She drinks avidly. He more slowly. Their hands are flat on the table.*)
(*Nevers.*)

SHE: The world moves along over my head. Instead of the sky . . . of course . . . I see the world walking. Quickly during the week. Slowly on Sunday. It doesn't know I'm in the cellar. They pretend I'm dead, dead a long way from Nevers. That's what my father wants. Because I'm disgraced, that's what my father wants.

(*Nevers: a father, a Nevers druggist, behind the window of his drug store.*)

HE: Do you scream?

(The room at Nevers.)

SHE: Not in the beginning; no, I don't scream: I call you softly.

HE: But I'm dead.

SHE: Nevertheless I call you. Even though you're dead. Then one day, I scream, I scream as loud as I can, like a deaf person would. That's when they put me in the cellar. To punish me.

HE: What do you scream?

SHE: Your German name. Only your name. I only have one memory left, your name.

(Room at Nevers, mute screams.)

SHE: I promise not to scream any more. Then they take me back to my room.

(*Room at Nevers. Lying down, one leg raised, filled with desire.*)

SHE: I want you so badly I can't bear it any more.

HE: Are you afraid?

SHE: I'm afraid. Everywhere. In the cellar. In my room.

HE: Of what?

(*Spots on the ceiling of the room at Nevers, terrifying objects at Nevers.*)

SHE: Of not ever seeing you again. Ever, ever.

(*They move closer together again, as at the beginning of the scene.*)

SHE: One day, I'm twenty years old. It's in the cellar. My mother comes and tells me I'm twenty. (*A pause, as if remembering.*) My mother's crying.

HE: You spit in your mother's face?

SHE: Yes.

(As if they were aware of these things together. He moves away from her.)

HE: Drink something.

SHE: Yes.

(He holds the glass for her to drink. She is worn out from remembering.)

SHE *(suddenly)*: Afterward, I don't remember any more. I don't remember any more . . .

HE *(trying to encourage her)*: These cellars are very old, and very damp, these Nevers cellars. . . . You were saying. . .

SHE: Yes. Full of saltpeter.

(Her mouth against the walls of the Nevers cellar, biting.)

SHE: Sometimes a cat comes in and looks. It's not a mean cat. I don't remember any more.

(A cat comes in the Nevers cellar and looks at this woman.)

SHE: Afterward, I don't remember any more.

HE: How long?

SHE *(still in a trancelike state)*: Eternity.

(Someone, a solitary man, puts a record of French bal-musette music on the juke box. To make the miracle of the lost memories of Nevers last, to keep anything from "moving," the Japanese pours the contents of his glass into hers.
In the Nevers cellar the cat's eyes and Riva's eyes glow.

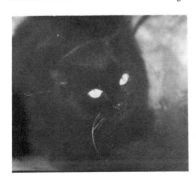 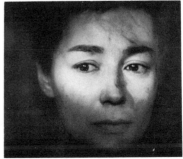

When she hears the music of the record she [*drunk or mad*] *smiles and screams:*)

SHE: Oh, how young I was, once!

(She comes back to Nevers, having hardly left it. She is haunted [*the choice of adjectives is voluntarily varied*].)

SHE: At night . . . my mother takes me down into the garden. She looks at my head. Every night she looks carefully at my head. She still doesn't dare come near me. . . . It's at night that I can look at the square, so I look at it. It's enormous *(gesturing)*! It curves in in the middle.

(The air shaft at the Nevers cellar. Through it, the rainbowlike wheels of bicycles passing at dawn at Nevers.)

SHE: Sleep comes at dawn.

HE: Does it rain sometimes?

SHE: . . . along the walls.

(She searches, searches, searches.)

SHE *(almost evil)*: I think of you, but I don't talk about it any
more.

(They move closer together again.)

HE: Mad.

SHE: Madly in love with you. *(Pause.)* My hair is growing back.
I can feel it every day, with my hand. I don't care. But nevertheless my hair is growing back . . . .

*(Riva in her bed at Nevers, her hand in her hair. She runs her
hands through her hair.)*

HE: Do you scream, before the cellar?

SHE: No. I'm numb.

(They are cheek-to-cheek, their eyes half-closed, at Hiroshima.)

SHE: They shave my head carefully till they're finished. They
think it's their duty to do a good job shaving the women's
heads.

HE *(very clearly)*: Are you ashamed for them, my love?

(The hair-cutting.)

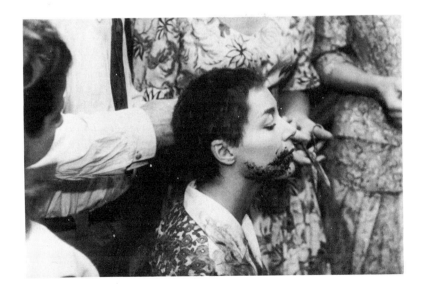

SHE: No. You're dead. I'm much too busy suffering. *(Dusk deepens. The following said with complete immobility:)* All I hear is the sound of the scissors on my head. It makes me feel a little bit better about . . . your death . . . like . . . like, oh! I can't give you a better example, like my nails, the walls . . . for my anger.

(She goes on, desperately against him at Hiroshima.)

SHE: Oh! What pain. What pain in my heart. It's unbelievable. Everywhere in the city they're singing the *Marseillaise*. Night falls. My dead love is an enemy of France. Someone says she should be made to walk through the city. My father's drug store is closed because of the disgrace. I'm alone. Some of them laugh. At night I return home.

(Scene of the square at Nevers. She screams, not words, but a formless scream understandable in any language as the cry of a child for its mother. He is still against her, holding her hands.)

HE: And then, one day, my love, you come out of eternity.

(The room at Nevers. Riva paces the floor. Overturns objects. Savage, conscious animailty.)

SHE: Yes, it takes a long time.
They told me it had taken a very long time.

At six in the evening, the bells of the St. Etienne Cathedral ring, winter and summer. One day, it is true, I hear them. I remember having heard them before—before—when we were in love, when we were happy.

I'm beginning to see.

I remember having already seen before—before—when we were in love, when we were happy.

I remember.

I see the ink.

I see the daylight.

I see my life. Your death.

My life that goes on. Your death that goes on

(Room and cellar Nevers.)

and that it took the shadows longer now to reach the corners of the room. And that it took the shadows longer now to reach the corners of the cellar walls. About half past six.

Winter is over.

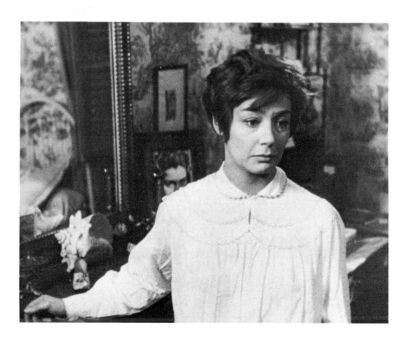

(A pause. Hiroshima. She is trembling. She moves away from his face.)

SHE: Oh! It's horrible. I'm beginning to remember you less clearly.

(He holds the glass and makes her drink. She's horrified by herself.)

SHE: ... I'm beginning to forget you. I tremble at the thought of having forgotten so much love ...
... More. *(He makes her drink again.)*

(She wanders. This time. Alone. He loses her.)

SHE: We were supposed to meet at noon on the quays of the Loire. I was going to leave with him. When I arrived at noon on the quay of the Loire, he wasn't quite dead yet. Someone had fired on him from a garden.

(The garden above the quay of the Loire. She becomes delirious, no longer looking at him.)

SHE: I stayed near his body all that day and then all the next night. The next morning they came to pick him up and they put him in a truck. It was that night Nevers was liberated. The bells of St. Etienne were ringing, ringing . . . Little by little he grew cold beneath me. Oh! how long it took him to die! When? I'm not quite sure. I was lying on top of him . . . yes . . . the moment of his death actually escaped me, because . . . because even at that very moment, and even afterward, yes, even afterward, I can say that I couldn't feel the slightest difference between this dead body and mine. All I could find between this body and mine were obvious similarities, do you understand? *(Shouting.)* He was my first love . . . .

(The Japanese slaps her. [Or, if you prefer, crushes her hands in his.] She acts as though she didn't know where it had come from. But she snaps out of it, and acts as though she realized it had been necessary.)

SHE: And then one day. . . I had screamed again. So they put me back in the cellar.

(Her voice resumes its normal rhythm. Here the entire scene of the marble that enters the cellar, the marble she picks up, the warm marble she encloses in her hand, etc., and that she gives back to the children outside, etc.)

SHE: . . . it was warm. . . .

(He lets her talk, without understanding. She goes on.)

SHE *(after a pause)*: I think then is when I got over my hate. *(Pause.)* I don't scream any more. *(Pause.)* I'm becoming reasonable. They say: "She's becoming reasonable." *(Pause.)* One night, a holiday, they let me go out.

(Dawn, at Nevers, beside a river.)

SHE: The banks of the Loire. Dawn. People are crossing the bridge, sometimes many, sometimes few, depending on the hour. From afar, it's no one.

(Republic Square, at Nevers, at night.)

SHE: Not long after that my mother tells me I have to leave for Paris, by night. She gives me some money. I leave for Paris, on a bicycle, at night. It's summer. The nights are warm. When I reach Paris two days later the name of Hiroshima is in all the newspapers. My hair is now a decent length. I'm in the street with the people.

(Someone puts another bal-musette record on the juke box.)

SHE *(as if she were waking up)*: Fourteen years have passed.

(He gives her something to drink. She drinks. She apparently becomes quite calm. They are emerging from the Nevers tunnel.)

SHE: I don't even remember his hands very well. . . . The pain, I still remember the pain a little.

HE: Tonight?

SHE: Yes, tonight, I remember. But one day I won't remember it any more. Not at all. Nothing.

SHE (*raising her head to look at him*): Tomorrow at this time I'll be thousands of miles away from you.

HE: Does your husband know about this?

SHE (*hesitating*): No.

HE: Then I'm the only one who does?

SHE: Yes.

(*He gets up, takes her in his arms, forcing her to get up too, and holds her very tightly, shockingly. People look at them. They don't understand. He is overwhelmingly happy. He laughs.*)

HE: I'm the only one who knows. No one else?

SHE (*closing her eyes*): Don't say any more.

(*She moves even closer to him. She raises her hand, and caresses his lips very lightly. Then, as if she were suddenly very happy:*)

SHE: Oh, how good it is to be with someone, sometimes.

(*They separate, very slowly, he sits back down again.*)

HE: Yes.

(*Somewhere a lamp goes out, either on the river bank or in the bar. She jumps. She withdraws her hand, which she had placed again on his lips. He hasn't forgotten the passing time.*)

HE: Tell me more.

SHE: All right.

(*Searches, can't find anything.*)

HE: Tell me more.

SHE: I want to have lived through that moment. That incomparable moment.

(*She drinks. He speaks, as though divorced from the present.*)

HE: In a few years, when I'll have forgotten you, and when other such adventures, from sheer habit, will happen to me, I'll remember you as the symbol of love's forgetfulness. I'll think of this adventure as of the horror of oblivion. I already know it.

(People enter the café. She looks at them.)

SHE: *(hopefully):* Doesn't anything ever stop at night, in Hiroshima?

(They begin a final game of mutual deception.)

HE: Never, it never stops in Hiroshima.

(She puts down her glass, smiles, her smiling concealing a feeling of distress.)

SHE: I love that . . . cities where there are always people awake, day or night. . . .

(The proprietress of the bar turns out a light. The record stops playing. They're in semi-darkness. The late but eluctable hour when the cafés close is fast approaching. They both close their eyes, as if seized by a feeling of modesty. The well-ordered world has thrown them out, for their adventure has no place in it. No use fighting. She suddenly understands this. When they raise their eyes again, they literally smile "in order not to cry." She gets up. He does nothing to restrain her. They are outside, in the night, in front of the café. She stands facing him.)

SHE: It's sometimes necessary to keep from thinking about these difficulties the world makes. If we didn't we'd suffocate.

(A last light goes out in the café. Both their eyes are lowered.)

SHE: Go away, leave me.

(He starts to leave, looks up at the sky.)

HE: It isn't daylight yet . . . .

SHE: *No. (Pause.)* Probably we'll die without ever seeing each other again.

HE: Yes, probably. *(Pause.)* Unless, perhaps, someday, a war. . . .

(Pause.)

SHE *(ironically):* Yes, a war. . . .

Part V

(After a further time lapse. We see her in the street, walking quickly. Then we see her in the lobby of the hotel. She takes her key. Then we see her on the stairway. Then we see her open the door to her room. Enter the room and stop short as before an abyss, or as if she had discovered someone already in the room. Then she backs out and closes the door softly.

Climbing the stairs, descending, going back up, etc. Retracing her steps. Coming and going in the hallway. Wringing her hands, searching for a solution, not finding it, returning to her room all of a sudden. And this time coming to terms with the room.

She goes to the basin, splashes water on her face. And we hear the first sentence of her interior dialogue:)

SHE: You think you know. And then, no. You don't.

In Nevers she had a German love when she was young. . . .

We'll go to Bavaria, my love, and there we'll marry.

She never went to Bavaria. *(Looking at herself in the mirror.)*

I dare those who have never gone to Bavaria to speak to her of love.

You were not yet quite dead.

I told our story.

I was unfaithful to you tonight with this stranger.

I told our story.

It was, you see, a story that could be told.

For fourteen years I hadn't found . . . the taste of an impossible love again.

Since Nevers.

Look how I'm forgetting you. . . .

Look how I've forgotten you.

Look at me.

73

(Through the open window we see the new Hiroshima, peacefully asleep. She suddenly raises her head, sees her wet face in the mirror—like tears—grown old, haggard. And this time, disgusted, she closes her eyes. She dries her face and quickly leaves, crossing the lobby.)

(When we see her again she is sitting on a bench, or on a pile of gravel, about fifty feet from the same bar where they had spent the evening together. The restaurant's light is in her eyes. Banal, almost empty: he is no longer there. She [lies down, sits down] on the gravel and continues to look at the café. [Now only one light is left on in the bar. The room where they had been a short while before is closed. The door into that room is slightly ajar, and by the dim light it is just possible to make out the arrangement of chairs and tables, which are no more than vague, vain shadows.]
She closes her eyes. Then opens them again. She seems to be asleep. But she is not. When she opens her eyes, she opens them suddenly. Like a cat. Then we hear her voice, an interior monologue:)

SHE: I'm going to stay in Hiroshima. With him, every night. In Hiroshima. *(Opening her eyes.)* I'm going to stay here. Here.

(She looks away from the café and gazes around her. Then suddenly she curls up as tightly as she can, a childlike movement, her head cuddled in her arms, her feet pulled up under her. The Japanese approaches her. She sees him, doesn't move, doesn't react. Their absence "from each other" has begun. No astonishment. He is smoking a cigarette.)

HE: Stay in Hiroshima.

SHE: *(glancing at him):* Of course I'm going to stay in Hiroshima, with you. *(She buries her head again and says, in a childish tone)*: Oh, how miserable I am. . . .

(He moves nearer to her.)

SHE: I never expected this would happen, really. . . . Go away.

HE *(moving away):* Impossible to leave you.

(We see them now on a boulevard. In the background, the lighted signs of nightclubs. The boulevard is perfectly straight. She is walking, he following. We see first one, then the other. Distress on both their faces. He catches up with her.)

HE *(softly)*: Stay in Hiroshima with me.

(She doesn't reply. Then we hear her voice in an interior monologue, loud and uncontrolled:)

SHE: He's going to come toward me, he's going to take me by the shoulders, he's-going-to-kiss-me. . . .

He'll kiss me . . . and I'll be lost. *(The word "lost" is said almost ecstatically.)*

(A shot of him. And we notice he's walking more slowly to let the distance between them grow. That instead of coming toward her he's moving farther away. She doesn't turn back.)

(A succession of streets in Hiroshima and Nevers. Riva's interior monologue.)

SHE: I meet you

I remember you.

This city was made to the size of love.

You were made to the size of my body.

Who are you?

You destroy me.

I was hungry. Hungry for infidelity, for adultery, for lies, hungry to die.

I always have been.

I always expected that one day you would descend on me.

I waited for you calmly, with infinite patience.

Take me. Deform me to your likeness so that no one, after you, can understand the reason for so much desire.

We're going to remain alone, my love.

The night will never end.

The sun will never rise again on anyone.

Never. Never more. At last.

You destroy me.

You're so good for me.

In good conscience, with good will, we'll mourn the departed day.

We'll have nothing else to do, nothing but to mourn the departed day.

And a time is going to come.

A time will come. When we'll no more know what thing it is that binds us. By slow degrees the word will fade from our memory.

Then it will disappear altogether.

(This time he accosts her face to face—for the last time—but from a distance. Henceforth she is inviolable. It is raining. They are under a store awning.)

HE: Maybe it's possible for you to stay.

SHE: You know it's not. Still more impossible than to leave.

77

HE: A week.

SHE: No.

HE: Three days.

SHE: Time enough for what? To live from it? To die from it?

HE: Time enough to know which.

SHE: That doesn't exist. Neither time enough to live from it. Nor time enough to die from it. So I don't give a damn.

HE: I would have preferred that you had died at Nevers.

SHE: So would I. But I didn't die at Nevers.

(She is seated on a bench in the waiting room of the Hiroshima railroad station. Still more time has elapsed. An elderly Japanese woman is seated beside her. Another interior monologue.)

SHE: Nevers, that I'd forgotten, I'd like to see you again tonight. Every night for months on end I set you on fire, while my body was aflame with his memory.

(Like a shadow the Japanese enters and sits on the same bench, on the opposite side of the old woman. He doesn't look at the French woman. His face is soaked from the rain. His lips are trembling slightly.)

SHE: While my body is still on fire with your memory, I would like to see Nevers again . . . the Loire.

(Shot of Nevers.)

Lovely poplar trees of Nièvre, I offer you to oblivion. *(The word "lovely" should be spoken like a word of love.)*
Three-penny story, I bequeath you to oblivion.

(The ruins at Nevers.)

One night without you and I waited for daylight to free me.

(The "marriage" at Nevers.)

One day without his eyes was enough to kill her.

Little girl of Nevers.

Shameless child of Nevers.

One day without his hands and she thinks how sad it is to love.

Silly little girl.

Who dies of love at Nevers.

Little girl with shaven head, I bequeath you to oblivion.

Three-penny story.

As it was for him, oblivion will begin with your eyes.

Just the same.

Then, as it was for him, it will encompass your voice.

Just the same.

Then, as it was for him, it will encompass you completely, little by little.

You will become a song.

(They are separated by the old Japanese woman. He takes a cigarette, rises slightly, and offers the French woman the package. "That's all I can do for you, offer you a cigarette, as I would offer one to anybody, to this old woman." She doesn't smoke. He offers the package to the old woman, lights her cigarette.
The Nevers forest moves past in the twilight. And Nevers. While the loudspeaker at the Hiroshima station blares: "Hiroshima, Hiroshima!" during the shots of Nevers.
The French woman seems to be asleep. The two Japanese beside her speak softly to keep from waking her up.)

THE OLD WOMAN: Who is she?

HE: A French woman.

THE OLD WOMAN: What's the matter?

HE: She's leaving Japan in a little while. We're sad at having to leave each other.*

---

*This exchange takes place in Japanese. Not translated in the film.

80

(She is gone. We see her again just outside the station. She gets into a taxi. Stops before a night club. "The Casablanca." Then he arrives after her.
She is alone at a table. He sits down at another table facing hers. It's the end. The end of the night which marks the beginning of their eternal separation. A Japanese who was in the room goes over to her and engages her in conversation.)

THE JAPANESE: Are you alone?†

(She replies only by signs.)

THE JAPANESE: Do you mind talking with me a little?

(The place is almost empty. People are bored.)

THE JAPANESE: It is very late to be lonely.

(She lets herself be accosted by another man in order to "lose" the one we know. But not only is that not possible, it's useless. For the other one is already lost.)

THE JAPANESE: May I sit down? Are you just visiting Hiroshima?
    Do you like Japan?
    Do you live in Paris?

---

†This passage in English in the film.

(We can see day beginning to break [through the windows]. The interior monologue has stopped. This unknown Japanese is talking to her. She looks at the other. The unknown Japanese stops talking to her. And then, terrifying, "the dawn of the damned" can be seen breaking through the windows of the night club.)

(She is next seen leaning against the door inside her hotel room. Her hand on her heart. A knock. She opens.)

HE: Impossible not to come.

(They are standing in the room, facing each other, their arms at their sides, their bodies not touching. The room is in order. The ash trays are empty. It is now full daylight. The sun is up. They don't even smoke. The bed is still made. They say nothing. They look at each other. The silence of dawn weighs on the whole city. He enters her room. In the distance, Hiroshima is still sleeping.

82

All of a sudden, she sits down. She buries her head in her hands, clenches her fist, closes her eyes, and moans. A moan of utter sadness. The light of the city in her eyes.)

SHE: I'll forget you! I'm forgetting you already! Look how I'm forgetting you! Look at me!

(He takes her arms [wrists], she faces him, her head thrown back. She suddenly breaks away from him. He helps her by an effort of self-abstraction. As if she were in danger. He looks at her, she at him, as she would look at the city, and suddenly, very softly, she calls him. She calls him from afar, lost in wonder. She has succeeded in drowning him in universal oblivion. And it is a source of amazement to her.)

SHE: Hi-ro-shi-ma.
Hi-ro-shi-ma. That's your name.

(They look at each other without seeing each other. Forever.)

HE: That's my name. Yes. Your name is Nevers. Ne-vers-in France.

THE END

APPENDICES

NOCTURNAL NOTATIONS

*(Notes on Nevers)**

ON THE SCENE OF THE
GERMAN'S DEATH

Both of them, equally, are possessed by this event: his death.

Neither of them is angry. They are only inconsolably sorry about their love.

The same pain. Same blood. Same tears.

The absurdity of war, laid bare, hovers over their blurred bodies.

One might believe her dead, so completely has his death drained all life from her.

He tries to caress her hips, as he had caressed her while making love. But he cannot.

It is as though she were helping him die. She doesn't think of herself, only of him. And he consoles her, almost apologizes for having to make her suffer, for having to die.

When she is alone, in the same spot where a short while before they were together, pain has not yet taken hold of her life. She is simply utterly amazed to find herself alone.

ON THE SHOT OF THE GARDEN FROM
WHICH THE GERMAN WAS FIRED UPON

They fired from this garden as they might have fired from any other garden in Nevers. From all the other gardens in Nevers.

Only chance has decided that it would be from this one.

This garden is henceforth marked by the sign of the banality of his death.

---

*Not in chronological order.

Its color and form are henceforth prophetic. It is from here that his death began, for all eternity.

A GERMAN SOLDIER CROSSES A PROVINCIAL
SQUARE DURING THE WAR

Late one afternoon a German soldier crosses a square somewhere in the provinces of France.

Even war is boring.

The German soldier crosses the square like a peaceful target.

We're in the depths of the war, the time when it seemed it would never end. People no longer pay any attention to the enemy. They've grown used to the war. The Champs de Mars Square reflects a quiet despair. The German soldier feels it too. We don't talk enough about the boredom of war. Within this boredom, women behind shutters watch the enemy walking across the square. Here adventure is circumscribed by patriotism. The other adventure must be strangled. Nevertheless, people watch. There's no crime in watching.

ON THE SHOTS DEALING WITH RIVA'S MEETINGS
WITH THE GERMAN SOLDIER

We kissed behind the ramparts. Deathly afraid, but utterly happy, I kissed my enemy.

The ramparts were always deserted during the war. During the war Frenchmen were shot there. And after the war, Germans.

I discovered his hands when they touched the gates to open them before me. I soon wanted to punish his hands. I bite them after making love.

It was inside the ramparts of the city that I became his wife.

I no longer remember the gate at the end of the garden. He waited for me there, sometimes for hours. Especially at night. Any time I could find a free moment. He was afraid.

I was afraid.

88

When we had to cross the city together I walked ahead of him, filled with fear. People lowered their eyes. We thought they were indifferent. We began to take more chances.

I asked him to walk across the square, behind the fence, so that I could see him once during the day. So every day he walked along the fence, letting me look at him.

In the ruins, in winter, the wind blows in eddies. The cold. His lips were cold.

AN IMAGINARY NEVERS

In my memory, Nevers, where I was born, is inseparable from myself.

It is a city a child can walk around.

Bounded on one side by the Loire river, on the other by the ramparts.

Beyond the ramparts lies the forest.

Nevers can be measured by a child's foosteps.

Nevers "exists" between the ramparts, the river, the forest, the countryside. The ramparts are imposing. The river is the broadest, the best-known, the most beautiful in France.

Thus Nevers is circumscribed like a capital.

When I was a little girl and walked all the way around Nevers, I thought it was enormous. Its shadows trembled in the Loire, making it still bigger.

For a long time I was still under the illusion that Nevers was enormous, until I was twelve or thirteen.

Then Nevers closed in on itself. It grew as one grows. I knew nothing about other cities. I needed a city the size of love itself. I found it in Nevers itself.

To say that Nevers is a small city is an error of the mind and heart. Nevers was enormous for me.

The wheat is at its gates. The forest is at its windows. At night owls come into the gardens, and you have to struggle to keep from being afraid.

At Nevers, more than anywhere else, they keep a close watch over love.

Lonely people await their death there. No other adventure except love can make them turn their attention from this vigil.

Thus in these tortuous streets the straight line of death's vigil lives.

Love is unpardonable there. At Nevers, love is the great sin. At Nevers, happiness is the great crime. Boredom, at Nevers, is a tolerated virtue.

Madmen walk in the outskirts. Bohemians. Dogs. And love.

To speak deprecatingly of Nevers would also be an error of the mind and heart.

ON THE SHOTS OF THE MARBLE
LOST BY THE CHILDREN

I screamed again. And that day I heard a scream. That last time that they put me in the cellar. The marble came toward me, taking its time, like an event.

Brightly colored rivers flowed inside it. Summer was inside the marble. And summer had also made it warm.

I already knew that one shouldn't eat things, eat any old thing, not the walls, not the blood of one's own hands nor the walls. I looked at it with tenderness. I placed it against my mouth, but didn't bite.

So much roundness, so much perfection, posed an insoluble problem.

Maybe I'll break it. I throw it, but it bounces back toward my hand. I do it again. It doesn't come back. It gets lost.

When it gets lost, something I recognize begins again. Fear returns. A marble can't die. I remember. I look. I find it again.

Children's shouts. The marble is in my hand. Shouts. Marble. It belongs to the children. No. They won't have it back. I open my hand. There it is, captive. I give it back to the children.

THE GERMAN SOLDIER COMES TO HAVE HIS
HAND BANDAGED AT THE DRUG STORE RIVA'S
FATHER OWNS

[In the middle of summer I wore (black) sweaters. At Nevers the summers are cold. The summers during the war. My father is bored. His shelves are empty. I obey my father like a child. I look at his burned hand. *I hurt him* as I bandage his hand. I raise my eyes and briefly meet his. They're light. He laughs because I hurt him. I don't laugh.]*

AN EVENING IN NEVERS DURING THE WAR.
FROM THE SQUARE
THE GERMAN SOLDIER WATCHES RIVA'S WINDOW

[My father drinks and is silent. I don't even know whether he's

---

*Bracketed sections in the Appendices refer to action omitted from the film.

listening to the music I'm playing. The evenings are deadly, but this is the first evening I realize it. The enemy raises his head toward me and smiles slightly. I feel as though I were witnessing a crime. I close the shutters as upon some loathsome scene.] In his armchair, my father is half-asleep, as usual. Our two plates and my father's wine are still on the table. Behind the shutters the square pounds like the sea, enormous. I go toward my father and from very close by—almost touching him—I look at him. A sleep induced by the wine. I hardly recognize my father.

A NEVERS EVENING

Alone in my room at midnight. From the Champs de Mars Square the sea still pounds beyond my shutters. He must have passed by again tonight. I didn't open my shutters.

THE MARRIAGE AT NEVERS

I became his wife in twilight, happiness, and shame. When it was over, darkness fell upon us. We didn't even notice it.

Shame had disappeared from my life. We were happy to see the night. I had always been afraid of night. That night was blacker than any I've ever seen since. My country, my city, my drunken father, were drowned in it. With the German occupation. In one fell swoop.

Black night of certainty. We watched it attentively, then seriously. Then one by one the mountains loomed up on the horizon.

ANOTHER NOTE ON THE GARDEN
FROM WHICH THE GERMAN WAS FIRED UPON

Love serves life by making dying easier.

This garden could make you believe in God.

This man, with his rifle, drunk with liberty, this unknown man of the end of July, 1944, this man of Nevers, my brother, how could he have known?

Riva herself makes no further comment when this scene appears.

To give any manifest sign of her pain would be to degrade the pain.

She has just discovered him, dying on the quay, in the sunlight. It is for the rest of us that the scene is unbearable. Not for Riva. Riva has stopped talking to us. She has, simply, stopped.

He is still alive.

Riva, on top of him, is at the extreme limit of pain. Madness

envelops her.

To see her smiling at him at this moment would even be logical.

Pain has its obscene side. Riva is obscene. Like a madwoman. She is no longer rational.

This was her first love. This is her first pain. We can scarcely look at Riva in this state. There's nothing we can do for her. Except wait. Wait until pain assumes a recognizable, decent shape in her.

Fresson dies. It is as if he were bound to the soil. Death took him completely by surprise. His blood flows like the river, and like time. Like sweat. He dies like a horse, with unsuspected strength. It occupies him almost completely. Then, when she comes, she brings tenderness with her, and the realization that it is useless to struggle against his death. A softness in Fresson's eyes. They smile. Yes. *You see, my love, even that was possible for us.* Funereal triumph. Fulfillment. I'm so sure I can't go on living after you die that I smile at you.

AFTER THE GERMAN SOLDIER'S BODY
HAS BEEN TAKEN AWAY IN A TRUCK
RIVA REMAINS ALONE ON THE QUAY

That day the sun was shining gloriously. But, as every day, twilight comes.

What remains of Riva, on this quay, is the beating of her heart. (Late in the afternoon it has rained. It has rained on Riva and on the city. Then the rain has stopped. Then Riva's head has been shaved. And on the quay, there remains the dry spot where Riva had been. Burned spot.)

It appears that she's asleep on the quay. She is scarcely recognizable. (Animals walk on her blood-stained hands.)

Dog?

RIVA'S PAIN. HER MADNESS.
THE NEVERS CELLAR

Riva still doesn't speak.

Summer wears on as if nothing had happened. All France is

celebrating. Amid joy and confusion.

The rivers also still flow as if nothing had happened. The Loire. Riva's eyes flow like the Loire, but *directed by pain,* amid this confusion.

The cellar is small as it might be large.

Riva screams as she might remain silent. She doesn't know she screams.

They punish her to teach her that she is screaming. Like a deaf person.

They have to teach her to hear when she screams.

They told her that later.

She scrapes her hands like an idiot. Birds, set free inside a house, clip their wings and don't feel anything. Riva makes her fingers bleed and then sucks her blood. Grimaces and begins again. One day, on a quay, she learned to love blood. Like an animal, a bitch. You really have to look at something. Riva isn't blind. She looks. She sees nothing. But she looks. People's feet let themselves be looked at.

The people who pass, pass in a necessary universe, yours and mine, in a span of time familiar to us.

Riva's looking at these people's feet (just as meaningful as their faces) takes place in an organic universe, whence reason has fled. She looks at a world of feet.

RIVA'S FATHER

The father is worn out by the war. He isn't a bad person, merely stupefied by what has happened to him, involuntarily. He is dressed in black.

RIVA'S MOTHER

The mother is a lively person. Considerably younger than the father. She loves her child more than anything in the world. When Riva screams, she becomes terribly upset about her. The mother is afraid they'll do something more to her daughter. She's in complete control of the household. A strong person. She doesn't want

95

Riva to die. She treats her child with rough tenderness. But an infinite tenderness. Contrary to the father, she hasn't given up hope for her daughter.

They take her down into the cellar as though she were ten years old. They are in black. Riva, between them, is dressed in a light color. A very young girl's lace-trimmed nightgown that her mother made, a mother who constantly forgets that her child is growing up.

RIVA IN THE NEVERS CELLAR
AND IN HER ROOM

Riva, completely white, is in a corner of the cellar. There, as everywhere else, always. Her eyes as they were beside the river. The eyes she had on the quay. Not guilty. Terrifying childhood.

It is at night that she becomes rational again. That she remembers she is someone's wife. She too has been completely subjugated by desire. That he is dead doesn't keep her from desiring him. She wants him so badly she can't bear it any longer, and he is dead. An exhausted body, breathing heavily. Her mouth is moist. Her pose is that of a lustful woman, immodest to the point of vulgarity. More immodest than anywhere else. Disgusting. She desires a dead man.

RIVA TOUCHES THE OBJECTS IN HER ROOM.
"I REMEMBER ALREADY HAVING SEEN. . ."

In this state anything can be seen by Riva. A whole collection of objects, or the objects taken separately. It hardly matters. Everything will be seen *by* her.

RIVA LICKS THE SALTPETER IN THE CELLAR

For lack of something better, saltpeter can be eaten. The salt of the stones. Riva eats the walls. She also kisses them. She is in a universe of walls. A man's memory is in these walls, one with the stone, the air, the earth.

A CAT ENTERS THE NEVERS CELLAR

The cat, always the same, comes into the cellar. Ready for any eventuality. Riva has completely forgotten that cats exist.

Cats are completely domesticated. They have generally pleasant dispositions. Their eyes are not tame. The cat's eyes and Riva's eyes look alike and stare at each other. Blankly. Almost impossible to outstare a cat. Riva can do it. Little by little she enters the stare of the cat. There is nothing else in the cellar except a single stare, the stare of the cat-Riva.

Eternity beggars description. It is neither beautiful nor ugly. Can it be a stone, the shining corner of some object? *The stare of a cat?* Everything at once? The cat is asleep. Riva is asleep. The cat with its eyes open. Inside the cat's stare or inside Riva's stare? Oval pupils, which fasten on nothing. Enormous pupils. Empty circuses. Where time beats.

THE SQUARE AT NEVERS SEEN BY RIVA

The square goes on. Where are these people going? They are rational. The bicycle wheels look like suns. What moves is more easily seen than what does not move. Bicycle wheels. Feet. The whole square moves.

Sometimes, it's the sea. Even fairly often, the sea. Later she'll realize that it is dawn she has mistaken for the sea. It makes her sleepy, dawn, the sea.

RIVA, LYING DOWN, HER HANDS IN HER HAIR

When she didn't die, her hair began to grow back. Life's obstinacy. At night, during the day, her hair grows. Secretly, under the silk handkerchief. I softly caress my head. It's nicer to touch. It doesn't prick the fingers any more.

WHEN RIVA'S HEAD WAS SHAVED AT NEVERS

They shaved her head.
They do it almost absent-mindedly. She had to be shaved. Let's

98

do it. We have plenty of other things to do somewhere else. But we're doing our duty.

A warm wind blows from the square to the spot where they shave her. And yet it is cooler here than anywhere else.

The girl whose head has been shaved is the druggist's daughter. She seems almost to offer her head to the scissors. She almost helps them with the operation, as though her automatism were already a fact. It's nice to have your head shaved, it makes it lighter. (She is covered with the locks of hair that have fallen upon her.)

They are shaving someone's head somewhere in France. Here it's the druggist's daughter. The wind bears the strains of the *Marseillaise* to the crowd and encourages the exercise of a hasty, ridiculous justice. They haven't time enough to be intelligent. This is a theater where there is no performance. None. Something might have been staged, but the performance failed to take place.

After she has been shaved, the girl still waits. She's at their disposal. The city was made to suffer. This compensates. Helps work up an appetite. This girl has to leave. It's ugly, maybe disgusting. Since she seems inclined to stay here, they have to chase her away. They chase her like a rat. But she can't climb the steps very fast, not fast enough to please them. It seems she's still waiting *for something else,* something that didn't happen. That she is almost disappointed to have to move, move her legs, walk. She finds that the ramp is made to help her do that.

AT MIDNIGHT RIVA GOES HOME WITH HER HEAD SHAVED

Riva watches her mother come toward her. Riva's expression seems to say, "To think you brought me into this world." A closer guess would be: "What does it mean?"

Perhaps Riva frowns slightly, asking the sky, her mother. She is at the *exact* limit of her strength. When her mother reaches her, she will have exceeded this limit and fall in her mother's arms as though she had fainted. But her eyes will still be open.

What happens then between Riva and her mother is purely physical. Her mother takes Riva skillfully. She knows her child's weight. Riva will put herself at that part of her mother's body where since childhood she's been used to waiting for her sorrows to subside.

Riva is cold. Her mother will rub her arms and back. She'll kiss her child's shaved head, *without realizing what she's doing.* Nothing pathetic, nothing. Her child is alive. Relatively speaking, that in itself is cause for rejoicing. She takes her home. She literally tears her away, she has to tear her away from that tree. *Riva is then as heavy as she'll be when she's dead.*

PORTRAIT OF RIVA.
THE RETURN OF REASON

She paces the floor. Time has passed.

Her madness is now restless. She has to move. She paces the floor. The circle is closing, but it's going to explode. It's in its final stages.

Riva's face is like plaster. *Her face hasn't been used for several months.* Her lips have become thin. Her expression can shrink. Her body no longer has any meaning. When she paces the floor, her body serves merely to bear her head. She still calls him, but more and more rarely, and slowly. The memory of a memory. Her body is dirty, *uninhabited.* She's going to be free, it will soon be over. The circle is going to explode. She's destroying an imaginary universe, overturning objects; looking at them inside out.

RIVA'S MADNESS

When she looks at the lower corners of the room and recognizes something, her lips tremble. Is she smiling or crying? Same thing. She's listening. One might think she's preparing some vile deed. But she's not. All she's doing is listening to the church bells of St.-Etienne. Complete consummation of pain. She listens to the sounds of the city. Then paces the floor again. All of a sudden she stretches. *Her renascent reason frightens her.* She tries to kick something away. What? Shadows.

Riva, like a flower, reaches the top of the stairway leading down to the quay.

A round, full skirt. The beginning of the thighs and breasts.

RIVA GOES OUT, AT DAWN,
ON THE QUAYS OF THE LOIRE

They let me go out. I'm terribly tired. Too young to suffer, they say. The weather is lovely, they say. Eight months already, they say. My hair is long. No one's passing. I'm not afraid any more. There. I don't know what I'm getting myself ready for. . . . My mother frets about my health for that purpose. I fret about my health. You shouldn't look too long at the Loire, they say. I'll look at it.

People are crossing the bridge. Banality is sometimes striking. This is peace, they say. They are the people who shaved me. No one has shaved me. This is the Loire that *takes* my eyes. I look at it, and can't take my eyes off it. I think of nothing, nothing. What order.

What order. I have to leave. I'm leaving. In a re-established order. Nothing more can happen to me except to exist. All right.

It's a nice night. I'm leaving the Loire. The Loire is still at the end of every road. Patience. The Loire will disappear from my life.

NEVERS

(As a reminder)

RIVA HERSELF TELLS OF HER LIFE AT NEVERS

At seven in the evening the cathedral of St.-Etienne tolled the hour. The drug store closed.

Raised in the war, I didn't pay too much attention to it, although my father talked to me about it every night.

I helped my father in the drug store. I was a druggist's assistant. I had just finished my studies. My mother* was living in the south of France. Several times during the year, over the holidays, I went to visit her.

At seven in the evening, winter and summer, during the black night of the occupation or during the sunny days of June, the drug store closed. It was always too soon for me. We went up to the rooms on the second floor. All—or almost all—the movies were German. I wasn't allowed to go to the movies. At night, beneath the windows of my room, the Champ de Mars loomed even bigger.

There was no flag on the town hall. I had to think back to my early childhood to remember the street lamps lighted.

They crossed the border between northern and southern France.

The enemy arrived. Germans crossed the Champs de Mars, singing, at fixed hours. From time to time one of them came to the drug store.

Then they imposed a curfew too.

Then came Stalingrad.

Men were shot along the ramparts.

---

*Riva's mother was either Jewish [or separated from her husband].

Other men were deported. Others fled to join the Resistance. Some remained here, growing rich and afraid. The black market was in full swing. The children of St.- . . . working-class suburb were starving to death, while at the "Great Stag" people ate goose liver.

My father gave medicines to the children of St.-. . . . I took them to them twice a week, on my way to my piano lesson, after the drug store was closed. Sometimes I was late getting back. My father was watching for me behind the shutters. Sometimes at night my father asked me to play the piano for him.

After I had finished playing, my father fell silent, again prey to despair. He was thinking of my mother.

After I had finished playing, in the evening, terror-stricken by the enemy, my youth rose up and overwhelmed me. I didn't say anything to my father about it. He said I was his only consolation.

The only men in the city were German. I was seventeen years old.

The war was interminable. My youth was interminable. I couldn't get away from the war, or from my youth.

My mind was already confused by different standards of morality.

For me Sunday was a holiday. I raced through the city on my bicycle and went to Ezy to get the butter necessary for my growth. I rode along the Nièvre. Sometimes I stopped under a tree and fumed about how long the war was. While I grew up hating the enemy. And the war. I always enjoyed seeing the river.

One day, a German soldier came to the drug store to have his burned hand bandaged. We were alone in the store. I bandaged his hand as I had been taught, filled with hate. The enemy thanked me.

He came back. My father was there and asked me to take care of him.

I bandaged his hand again in my father's presence. I kept my eyes lowered, as I had been taught.

And yet, that evening, I felt especially fed up with the war. I said so to my father. He didn't reply.

I played the piano. Then we turned out the lights. He had asked me to close the shutters.

On the square, a young German with a bandaged hand was

leaning against a tree. I recognized him in the darkness because of the white spot his hand made. It was my father who closed the window. I knew that for the first time in my life a man had listened to me play the piano.

The man came back the next day. Then I saw his face. How could I keep from looking at him again? My father came toward us. He pushed me aside and told the enemy soldier that his hand didn't require any further attention.

That evening my father asked me expressly not to play the piano. At dinner he drank much more wine than usual. I obeyed my father. I thought that he'd gone a little crazy. I thought he was either drunk or crazy.

My father was in love with my mother, really in love. He still loved her. He suffered terribly at being separated from her. Now that she was no longer here, he had begun to drink.

Sometimes he went to see her, leaving me in charge of the drug store.

He left the following day, without mentioning the previous day's incident again.

The day after he left was a Sunday. It was raining. I was going to the farm at Ezy. As usual, I stopped under a poplar tree, beside the river.

Not long afterward the enemy stopped under the same poplar tree. He was also riding a bicycle. His hand was all better.

He didn't leave. The rain was falling, a heavy rain. Then the sun came out, while it was still raining. He stopped looking at me, smiled, and asked me to notice how sometimes, in summer, the sun and the rain can be together.

I didn't say anything. And yet I looked at the rain.

Then he told me that he had followed me here. That he wouldn't leave.

I left. He followed me.

For a whole month he followed me. I didn't stop any more beside the river. Never. But he was always there, every Sunday. How could I ignore the fact that he was there for me?

I said nothing about it to my father.

I began to dream of an enemy, at night, during the day. And in my dreams morality and immorality were so intertwined that soon

I couldn't tell one from the other. I was twenty.

One evening, in the St.-. . . . suburb, while I was turning a corner, someone grabbed me by the shoulders. I hadn't seen him come. It was night, half past eight, in July. It was the enemy.

We met in the woods. In barns. In the ruins. And then in rooms.

One day my father received a poison pen letter. The debacle was beginning. It was July, 1944. I denied everything.

It was under the same poplar trees bordering the river that he told me he was leaving. . . . He was leaving the next morning by truck for Paris. He was happy because it was the end of the war. He talked to me about Bavaria, where I was to join him. Where we were supposed to be married.

There was already some sporadic shooting in the city. People were ripping down their black curtains. Radios were blaring day and night. Fifty miles away, German convoys lay stranded in gullies.

I excluded this enemy from all the others.

It was my first love.

I couldn't see any difference at all now between his body and mine. All I could see was an extraordinary similarity between his body and mine.

His body had become mine, I was no longer capable of distinguishing it. I had become the living denial of reason. And how I would have swept aside all the good reasons they might have given as arguments against my lack of reason, swept them aside like so many houses made of cards, yes, like so many imaginary reasons. And may those who have known what it means to lose control of themselves throw the first stone at me. My only allegiance was to love itself.

I had left a note for my father. I told him that the poison pen letter had told the truth: that for six months I had been in love with a German soldier. That I wanted to follow him to Germany.

At Nevers, the Resistance was already sniping at the enemy. The police had disappeared. My mother returned.

He was leaving the next day. It was agreed that he would take me in his truck, under the camouflage netting. We thought we'd never have to be separated again.

We went once again to the hotel. He left at dawn to rejoin his unit, in the direction of Saint-Etienne.

We were supposed to meet at noon, on the quay of the Loire. When I arrived, at noon, on the quay of the Loire, he wasn't quite dead yet. They had fired on him from a garden above the quay.

I spent all day lying on his body, and all that night.

The next day they came to take him away, and they put him on a truck. It was during that night that the city was liberated. The bells of Saint-Etienne filled the city. I think, yes, I think I heard them.

They put me in a warehouse at the Champs de Mars. There, some of them said I would have to be shaved. I didn't care. The sound of the scissors on my head left me utterly indifferent. When it was over, a man about thirty years old led me into the street. There were six of them around me. They were singing. I didn't feel anything.

My father, behind the shutters, must have seen me. The drug store was closed for reasons of family disgrace.

They took me back to the same warehouse at the Champs de Mars. They asked me what I wanted to do. I said I didn't care. Then they told me to go home.

It was midnight. I climbed over the garden wall. It was a beautiful night. I lay down on the grass to die. But I didn't die. I was cold.

For a long time I called my mother. . . . About two in the morning there were lights in the shutters.

They pretended I was dead. And I lived in the cellar of the drug store.. I could see the people's feet, and at night the vast sweep of the Champs de Mars Square.

I went mad. Out of spite. I spit in my mother's face, it seems. I have only hazy memories of this period while my hair was growing out. Except the memory of spitting in my mother's face.

Then, little by little, I could tell the difference between day and night. I could tell that the shadow reached the corner of the cellar walls about half past four, and, once, that winter was over.

At night, late, they sometimes let me go out wrapped up in a cape. Alone. On my bicycle.

It took my hair a year to grow back. I still think that if the people who shaved my head had remembered how long it takes for hair to grow back, they would have thought twice about shaving me. It was by a lack of the men's imagination that I was disgraced.

One day my mother came to feed me, as she was accustomed to doing. She told me the time had come for me to leave. She gave me some money.

I left for Paris on my bicycle. It was a long way, but the weather was warm. Summer. When I reached Paris, the morning of the second day, the word Hiroshima was in all the newspapers. It was extraordinary news. My hair was now a decent length. No one was shaved.

PORTRAIT OF THE JAPANESE

He's a man of about forty. Tall. With a fairly "Western" face.

The choice of a Western-looking Japanese actor should be interpreted in the following way:

A Japanese actor with pronounced Japanese features might lead people to believe that it is especially because the protagonist is Japanese that the French actress was attracted to him. Thus, whether we liked it or not, we'd find ourselves caught again in the trap of "exoticism," and the involuntary racism inherent in any exoticism.

The spectator should not say: "How attractive Japanese men are," but "How attractive *that man* is."

This is why it is preferable to minimize the difference between the two protagonists. If the audience never forgets that this is the story of a Japanese man and a French woman, the profound implications of the film are lost. If the audience does forget it, these profound implications become apparent.

Monsieur Butterfly is outmoded. So is Mademoiselle de Paris. We should count upon the equalitarian function of the modern world. And even cheat in order to show it. Otherwise, what would be the use of making a Franco-Japanese film? This Franco-Japanese film should *never* seem *Franco-Japanese,* but *anti-Franco-Japanese.* That would be a victory.

His profile might almost seem French. A high forehead. A large mouth. Full, but hard lips. Nothing affected or fragile about his face. No angle from which his features might seem vague (indecisive).

In short, he is an "international" type. What makes him attractive should be immediately apparent to everyone as being that quality found in men who have reached maturity without succumbing prematurely to fatigue, without having resorted to subterfuge.

He is an engineer. He is involved in politics. Not by chance.

109

The techniques are international. The game of political coordinates is too. He is a modern man, wise in the ways of the world. He would not feel out of place in any country in the world.

He coincides with his age, both physically and morally.

He hasn't "cheated" with life. He hasn't had to: he is a man who has always been interested in his own existence, and always sufficiently interested not to "trail in his wake" a nostalgic longing for adolescence, which so often makes men of forty those false young men still looking for what they should really do to *appear* sure of themselves. If he isn't sure of himself, it's for good reason.

He's not really a dandy, but neither is he careless about his appearance. *He is not a libertine.* He has a wife he loves, and two children. And yet he likes women. But he's never made a career as a "lady's man." He believes that that sort of career is a career of contemptible "substitution" and most suspect. That anyone who has never known the love of a single woman has never really known what it is to love, has perhaps never even attained real manhood.

It's for this very reason that his affair with the young French woman is a real love affair, even though it's a chance adventure. It's because he doesn't believe in the virtue of chance affairs that he can live this one with such sincerity, with such violence.

PORTRAIT OF THE FRENCH WOMAN

She's thirty-two.

She's more seductive than beautiful.

She too might be called in a certain way "The Look." Everything about her—her words, her movements—is manifest in her expression.

This look is not self-conscious. She looks for the sake of looking. Her look doesn't define her conduct, it *always* exceeds it.

No doubt all women have beautiful eyes when making love. But love throws this woman's soul into greater confusion (the choice of the term is voluntarily Stendhalian) than it does with most women, because she is "more in love with love itself" than most women are.

She knows people don't die of love. In the course of her life she's had a wonderful opportunity to die of love. She didn't die at Nevers. Since then, and till now at Hiroshima, where she meets this Japanese, she carries within her, with her, this vague yearning that marks a reprieved person faced with a unique chance to determine her own fate.

It's not the fact of having been shaved and disgraced that marks her life, it's the already mentioned defeat: the fact that she didn't die of love on August 2, 1944, on the banks of the Loire.

This is not in contradiction with her attitude at Hiroshima with the Japanese. On the contrary, this has a direct bearing on her attitude with the Japanese. . . . What she tells the Japanese is this lost opportunity which has made her what she is.

The story she tells of this lost opportunity literally transports her outside herself and carries her toward this new man.

To give oneself, body and soul, that's it.

That is the equivalent not only of amorous possession, but of a *marriage*.

She gives this Japanese—*at Hiroshima*—her most precious possession: herself as she now is, her *survival* after the death of her love *at Nevers*.